TO ALL THE VICTIMS OF BULLYING. Bullying is a fear, and we fear things we don't understand. Knowledge of these fears will open the doors of understanding. Remember, we all could become a bully, so think fondly of each other and choose your paths wisely.

Love You,
Jeni, Charlie Ray, and Dutchess Sharpe; the Robinson family; and Uncle Jerry (the original Dog Whisperer).

In loving memory of Viola Britt Harrell and Harry & Zelda Robinson.

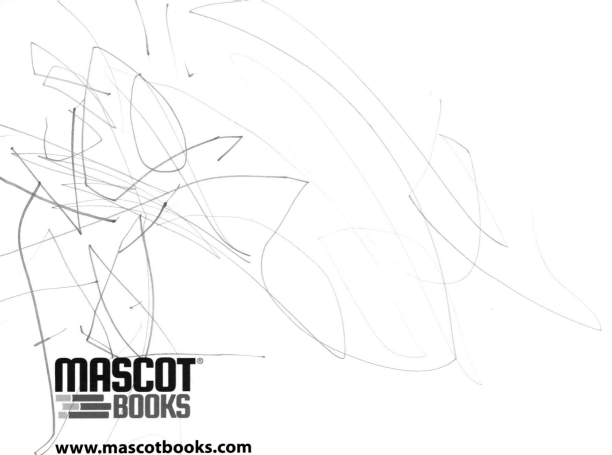

MASCOT® **BOOKS**

www.mascotbooks.com

PENELOPE'S BULLY

Second Printing. This Mascot Books edition printed in 2021.

For more information, please contact:
Mascot Books
620 Herndon Parkway, Suite 320
Herndon, VA 20170
info@mascotbooks.com

Library of Congress Control Number: 2020904636

CPSIA Code: PRT0221B
ISBN-13: 978-1-63177-462-1

Printed in the United States

PENELOPE'S
BULLY

ANDRE GATLING
Illustrated by Agus Prajogo

PENELOPE IS THE NEW KID on the block and doesn't know very many people. Her mother, Ms. Zelda, suggests, "Why don't you go to the playground and try to make some friends in our new neighborhood?"

When Penelope gets to the playground, she immediately realizes that the neighborhood kids are not very friendly. Some make fun of Penelope because she is different than everybody else, and someone even yells, "Ewww! Penelope!? WHAT KIND OF NAME IS THAT!?"

Upset, Penelope leaves the playground and sees a homeless dog sifting through a trash can. She remembers what she had been taught about meeting a stray dog: **BE STILL AND CALM**, don't try to touch the dog, and don't invade its space.

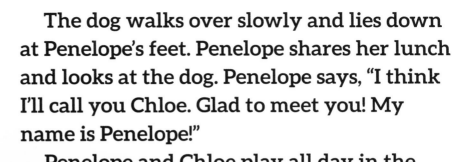

The dog walks over slowly and lies down at Penelope's feet. Penelope shares her lunch and looks at the dog. Penelope says, "I think I'll call you Chloe. Glad to meet you! My name is Penelope!"

Penelope and Chloe play all day in the park until Penelope comes up with a bright idea. "Why don't you come home with me, Chloe? **WOULD YOU LIKE THAT?**"

Penelope goes home and asks her mom if Chloe can stay with them. Ms. Zelda says, "Well, we have to call THE ANIMAL SHELTER to see if anyone claims her." Until then, Ms. Zelda agrees that Chloe can stay as long as Penelope does all of her chores plus feeds, walks, and plays with Chloe every day.

Penelope agrees, and Chloe is so happy to have a new home that she does her **CHLOE DANCE!**

Penelope and Chloe have so much fun, and Chloe even helps with Penelope's chores. Chloe loves her new family so much; she spends time watching game shows with Ms. Zelda and scary movies with Penelope.

Penelope decides to take Chloe out and show her around the new neighborhood, but the new neighbors are **NOT TOO HAPPY.** The neighbors are terrified of Chloe because she is a pit bull. Penelope tries to tell everybody that Chloe is a good dog and just wants to be loved, but the neighbors don't buy it. They say that all **BULLIES** need to be taken to the shelter and locked away for good.

Chloe is so confused, and Penelope is so sad. They go home to Ms. Zelda, who reassures them, "Everything is going to be okay. Sometimes children and adults can be very mean when they don't know you or understand who you really are. Always be good, no matter how bad the people are around you.

"NEVER JUDGE WITHOUT FIRST UNDERSTANDING."

Encouraged, Penelope and Chloe return to the playground for a game of fetch.

At the playground, the neighborhood kids are having fun when suddenly, The Bullies appear! They are the three meanest kids in the neighborhood who tease and pick on all the other kids. They have three mean dogs named Rocket, Griffin, and Shadow. The kids start screaming, "Run! The Bullies are coming! **THE BULLIES ARE COMING!**"

Penelope and Chloe notice that the neighborhood kids are being picked on. Chloe sprints to help the kids but trips and spins in the air like a bowling ball, accidentally falling on Rocket, Shadow, and Griffin!

The rest of the Bullies run away scared, and all the children cheer her on, "Yay! **CHLOE SAVED US FROM THE BULLIES!**"

The kids and parents are so excited that they pick Penelope and Chloe up on their shoulders and parade them around the playground. Everyone tells Penelope how great Chloe is and that she should bring Chloe around more often.

Penelope and Chloe go home to tell Ms. Zelda how they made friends with the new kids, when Ms. Zelda answers a knock at the door. "Hello, my name is Mr. Harry, and I'm a dog catcher from Animal Control. I'm responding to a complaint about a pit bull residing here. I need to take her away to the shelter and make sure she's not a danger to society."

Penelope starts crying and begs, "Please don't take her away! She's my best friend, and she's not a danger. Please don't take her, please!" Chloe looks so scared and confused, but Mr. Harry takes her away. She goes to the place dogs call **THE BIG HOUSE**.

When Chloe arrives at The Big House, she meets Jordan, who sleeps in the cell next to her. "Dis is da Big House, Shorty! Where humans take in the mutts dat don't have a home, and where they put bad dogs away, too," Jordan tells her.

Chloe responds, "But I'm not a bad dog! I have a home where people love me, and I love them!"

Just then, an older, veteran pit bull named Cinnamon says, "HUMANS THINK ALL PIT BULLS ARE BAD, li'l one, even when we're just trying to protect someone or ourselves. A long time ago in the early 1800s, our great, great, great grandparents were trained to be fighters. But we grew tired of fighting and evolved into what HUMANS WOULD LATER CALL US—THEIR NANNY DOGS."

IDENTITY

NAME :
JORDAN
SEX :
FEMALE
BREED :
PITBULL

Jordan interrupts, "Yeah, yeah, Shorty. Pit bulls are some of the greatest babysitters and protectors in the world. We even served in the armed forces for humans!"

Cinnamon agrees, "That's correct. We served and were even used in Army recruitment posters during World War I, but the humans only remember the bad things pit bulls do. That scares them, no matter if the good outweighs the bad. **THAT'S WHY THEY CALL US BULLIES.**"

IDENTITY

NAME :
CINNAMON
SEX :
FEMALE
BREED :
PITBULL

IDENTITY

NAME :
CHLOE
SEX :
FEMALE
BREED :
PITBULL

Chloe is confused. She says, "BUT, I'M NOT A BULLY. All I did was try to protect the kids from some other bad dogs and mean kids."

Cinnamon reminds Chloe, "When you growl, bark, or worse—bite—humans become more scared than when other dogs do the same because of our fighting history. Humans don't understand that PIT BULLS ARE THE SAME AS ANY OTHER DOG.

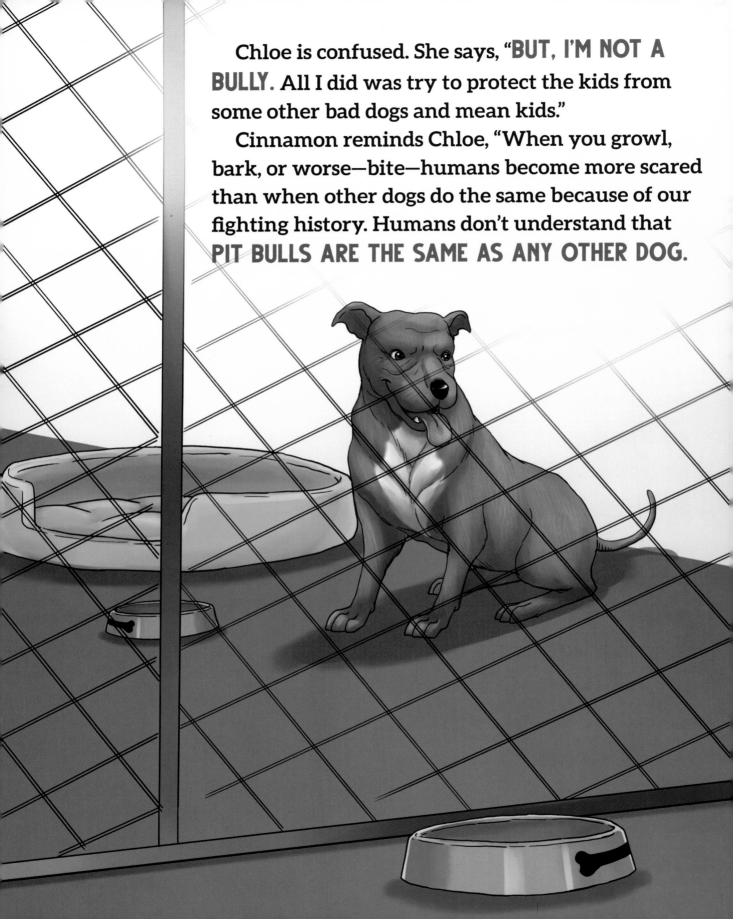

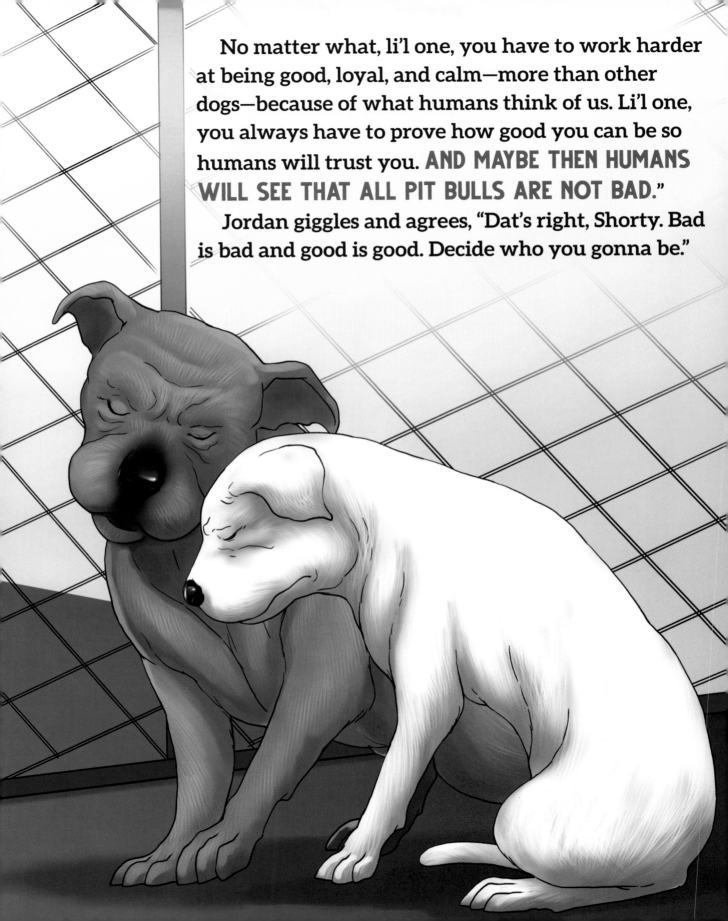

No matter what, li'l one, you have to work harder at being good, loyal, and calm—more than other dogs—because of what humans think of us. Li'l one, you always have to prove how good you can be so humans will trust you. **AND MAYBE THEN HUMANS WILL SEE THAT ALL PIT BULLS ARE NOT BAD.**"

Jordan giggles and agrees, "Dat's right, Shorty. Bad is bad and good is good. Decide who you gonna be."

Penelope and her new friends walk into the shelter and meet Mr. Harry. "Mr. Harry, **PLEASE LET CHLOE GO.** She was just trying to protect us from the bullies!"

Mr. Harry asks, "Do you promise to train Chloe to always be GOOD, OBEDIENT, AND CALM?"

Penelope answers, "I promise, Mr. Harry! I promise!"

"Well, wait right here and let me think about it," Mr. Harry says.

Back inside the shelter, Cinnamon says to Chloe, "You alone can change opinions about pit bulls because you are a good girl."

Chloe answers, "But how can I change what humans think about us all by myself?"

Cinnamon takes a long, deep breath, and a tear runs down her nose. "WITH LOVE, LI'L ONE, ONE HUMAN AT A TIME!"

Penelope waits outside anxiously, and the neighborhood kids wonder if they'll ever see Chloe again. Suddenly, Chloe bursts through the front doors and runs into Penelope's arms, **WAGGING HER TAIL FRANTICALLY WITH HAPPINESS.**

Mr. Harry looks at Penelope and says, "No one has claimed Chloe, so she is officially yours. But you have to promise to **TAKE GOOD CARE OF HER AND LOVE HER ENDLESSLY.**"

Chloe runs back to a window in the shelter to say goodbye to Cinnamon. She says, "I'll always remember what you taught me, and I'll be back to help you all find a home, too."

Cinnamon smiles. "Don't worry about that, li'l one. You've already given me hope and a home in your heart! GO ON NOW, AND BE A GOOD PIT BULL, CHLOE!"

IDENTITY

NAME :
JORDAN
SEX :
FEMALE
BREED :
PITBULL

ABOUT THE AUTHOR

Andre Gatling has had a long and successful career in the entertainment business as a stand-up comedian, among other roles. But his real love in life is rescuing and training an array of animals, particularly pit bulls.

Andre has spent well over twenty-five years working with animals and much more time growing up around pit bulls. He realized he had a unique approach to changing the behavior of aggressive dogs from his personal experiences with dogs and his time working with quarantined dogs in animal shelters. In his own words, Andre will tell you, "Aggression in a dog is similar to aggression in a human. We're both scared of what we don't understand, and our need to protect leads to aggression. Changing that aggression in a dog is more complex because the dog doesn't speak English, so I had to learn to speak dog."

Andre lives in Potomac Falls, Virginia with his two pit bulls, Chloe and Jordan, both of whom have American Kennel Club (AKC) accreditations. Chloe—who Andre calls a Ball Addict—has an AKC Canine Good Citizenship Title, while Jordan—who he calls the Bone Collector—achieved her AKC Star Puppy Award. These accolades help Andre's advocacy for pit bulls to help change the perception of the breed.